llama llama™
hooray for
new friends!

Based on the bestselling children's book
series by Anna Dewdney

 A GOLDEN BOOK · NEW YORK

Copyright © Anna E. Dewdney Literary Trust.
Copyright © 2023 Genius Brands International, Inc. Published in the United States by Golden Books,
an imprint of Random House Children's Books, a division of Penguin Random House LLC,
1745 Broadway, New York, NY 10019, and in Canada by Penguin Random House Canada Limited,
Toronto. Golden Books, A Golden Book, A Little Golden Book, the G colophon, and the distinctive
gold spine are registered trademarks of Penguin Random House LLC.
rhcbooks.com
Educators and librarians, for a variety of teaching tools, visit us at RHTeachersLibrarians.com
ISBN 978-0-593-56938-2 (trade) — ISBN 978-0-593-56939-9 (ebook)
Printed in the United States of America
10 9 8 7 6 5 4 3 2 1

One day, Llama Llama asks his mom if he can ride his bike with Gilroy.

"Another time," says Mama. "We're off to meet the new neighbors!"

"Do we have to?" asks Llama Llama.

"You'll have plenty of chances to ride with your friends," says Mama. "Right now we have to welcome new ones to the neighborhood."

Inside, Mama Llama prepares treats for the new neighbors. She explains that taking food or a gift to new neighbors makes them feel welcome. That's what everyone did when she and Llama Llama were the new neighbors.

Llama Llama feels nervous, but Mama tells him not to worry about the new neighbors.

"Hi, Mr. and Mrs. Antelope," says Mama. "We're the Llamas. We wanted to welcome you to the neighborhood with some treats."

The Antelopes invite the Llamas inside. They tell Mama and Llama Llama that they just moved from the city.

"Llama Llama, you should meet our daughter, Audrey," says Mr. Antelope. "She's just about your age."

He takes Llama Llama to Audrey's room.

"Hi, nice to meet you," says Llama Llama.

Llama Llama can't help noticing that Audrey's arm and leg look different from his.

"What happened there?" he asks.

Audrey explains that she was born this way, but that it doesn't slow her down at all.

"Actually, my leg is springy, so it helps me jump high when I'm playing basketball," she says.

"You play basketball?" asks Llama Llama.

"Soccer, too!" says Audrey.

When it's time to go home, Llama Llama notices Audrey's bike. It's just like his! Mama encourages Llama Llama to invite Audrey to go riding with him and his friends that afternoon, but Llama Llama isn't so sure.

"Maybe we can have that playdate in a day or two," he says.

"A playdate sounds really good!" says Audrey.

That afternoon, Llama Llama rides bikes with Gilroy and Luna. Gilroy asks what the new neighbor is like. "She's nice," says Llama Llama. "But she's busy unpacking, so she couldn't ride with us today."

Just then, Mama calls Llama Llama over.
"You seem to feel uncomfortable around Audrey," she says.

"What if Luna likes Audrey better than me and just wants to play with her? What if all my friends do?" asks Llama Llama.

"Your friends will always be your friends," says Mama. "You have to think about Audrey's feelings. She doesn't know anyone in our town."

Llama Llama realizes that Mama is right. "If it's not too late, maybe she'll come riding with us now," he says.

Llama Llama goes back to Audrey's house.

"Sorry I didn't invite you earlier," he tells her. "I know it must be hard to be new in the neighborhood. Do you want to come riding with all of us today?"

"I definitely do!" says Audrey.

Audrey joins Llama Llama and his friends.
"Your leg looks super springy," Gilroy tells Audrey.
"It is!" says Audrey. "It's great for bike riding."
"Oh, yeah?" says Gilroy. "Wanna race?"

Gilroy and Audrey ride as fast as they can. It's a close race, but Audrey wins.

"That was super fun, Audrey!" says Gilroy.

"It's so awesome to be able to ride my bike around like this," says Audrey. "There was way too much traffic in the city we moved from."

The friends decide to show Audrey some of the other places in town to ride in.

"The pond is one of my favorite places to ride around," says Llama Llama. "And the park is my favorite," says Luna.

Just then, they run into Nelly and Euclid.
"This is Audrey, our new friend," says
Llama Llama.
"Welcome, Audrey!" say Nelly and Euclid.
"Have you seen downtown yet?" asks Nelly.
Audrey says no.

Together, the friends ride downtown. They show Audrey the grocery store, the bookstore, and the toy store.
"Thank you all for showing me around and for making me feel welcome," says Audrey.

"We're not done yet," says Nelly. "Let's go to the best place in town— my dad's bakery!"

At the bakery, Audrey is amazed at all the cookies, cakes, and pastries! Nelly's dad gives Audrey a warm cookie, fresh from the oven.

"Thank you so much!" says Audrey. She takes a big bite and smiles. "It tastes as good as it smells."

Soon it's time for Gilroy's soccer game.
But there's a problem.
    "We need one more player," says Gilroy.
    "Audrey plays soccer!" says Llama Llama.
    "Great—let's go!" says Gilroy.

At the game, Audrey does great.
She even scores the winning goal!

Audrey's new friends cheer from the sidelines.

"It's like she's been here all along," says Llama Llama.